ISBN (Paperback): 979-8-9891177-5-8
ISBN (eBook): 979-8-9891177-4-1

To my Aussie friends.

With,

Thank you to my Savior,
who rescued me many times.

Skip, the little kangaroo, and his best friend, Olivia, the koala, were playing hopscotch by the ocean.

Ian, the cockatoo, flew by and said, "G'day, mate. Something is happening at the beach."

"Let's go see," said the curious kangaroo.

They watched people in the water standing on boards on top of the waves.

"That looks fun!" said Skip.

Julie, the ostrich, was walking by and asked, "What is that?"

"No idea," said Olivia.

"I'm headed to the billabong for a dip," said the ostrich and kept walking.

That night, Skip was very excited. He said, "Mum, I want to go in the water and stand on the waves."

His baby sister Carmen looked at him with a binky in her mouth.

His mother said, "Skip, dear, you must not go in the water. You do not know how to swim. It is very dangerous, and I do not want anything to happen to you."

Before Skip fell asleep, he dreamed he was in the water, on the waves.

He was happy and said, "Ahhhhh."

The next day, Skip and Olivia talked about getting the kangaroo into the water.

Ted, the traveling turtle, walked by. He said, "How ya going?"

"I want to get in the water, but Mum said it is not a good idea. I want to be on the waves," said Skip.

The old turtle said, "I have traveled the world and seen amazing things, lad. If you want to do that, you must try."

The wise turtle slowly walked away.

But where does Skip start?

Then they meet James, the anteater. He was eating a salad because he is a veggo, "Yum, want some?" he asked.

"Naur," Skip and Olivia said, "We're trying to find something for Skip to stand on in the water."

"Oh, my little friends can help," said the anteater.

They found a fallen tree, and the red ants
went to work.

The ants chewed the wood to make a board
for Skip to stand on.

"Bonzer!" they all said.

Skip went out into the ocean and stood on the board.

A big wave flipped him over.

Splash!

Oh, No! Skip did not know how to swim!

A blue whale saw him, jumped out of the water,
And flipped Skip on his back. The kangaroo
floated back to land.

Someone was watching.

When Skip got out of the water, he said,
"Well, that did not go so well."

"Worth a shot," the koala said.

The next day, they went to the billabong, where their friends met.

Nathan, the crocodile, said, "What are you doing with that?"

"I want to stand on the waves," the kangaroo said.

Lauren, the platypus, said, "Skip, it's best if you stay on land; the water is not safe for you."

"Maybe I try water without waves," Skip said.

He went into the billabong, got on the board, hopped, and sank.

Splash!

"Crikey!" yelled the crocodile.

Ras and his dad Doc, the Wombats, were walking by and saw this.

"What are you doing, mate? You will hurt yourself and need to be rescued," Doc said.

Then Ras said, "We must go put out a bushfire. Skip, do not go near the water."

The others were talking about the little kangaroo.

"Why does he want to get in the water? He does not know how to swim."

"He is awfully silly," they all said.

The kangaroo and the koala returned to
the beach, and the surfer saw them. She waved
to Skip to come closer.

She handed the kangaroo a board and told
him to follow.

He went into the water but could not help
but hop and fall.

Splash!

They were not giving up. The surfer brought a bigger board.

She tied a rope to Skip's leg, and they went into the water. The kangaroo did not fall off the board and stood on the waves.

"Cowabunga," shouted Olivia.

Skip was surfing!

If he fell into the water, he would float on his back.

The surfer told him to return the next day for something special.

Skip was stoked and had a surprise to share.

Ian, the cockatoo, flew around and told the others to go to the beach to watch the kangaroo in the water.

When they heard about this, they were shocked.

Was the kangaroo taking a risk?

They went to the beach and saw Skip on a big board riding a huge wave in the ocean.

Skip was in a surfing competition,
and he was winning!

The others were happy for Skip because the little kangaroo did not give up his dreams.

They shouted and cheered,
"Gnarly! Surf Skip surf!"

I hope you enjoyed the book and
that it encourages you to share love and
chase dreams.

For more inspirational books in the series,
visit: www.vatsanabooks.com.

Printed in the USA
CPSIA information can be obtained
at www.ICGtesting.com
JSHW040545011123
51233JS00011B/234